PUFFIN BOOKS

Sky Horses

Cloud Magic

The first book in the quartet

Linda Chapman lives in Leicestershire with her family and two Bernese mountain dogs. When she is not writing, she spends her time looking after her two young daughters and baby son, horse riding and talking to people about writing.

You can find out more about Linda on her websites at *lindachapman.co.uk* and *lindachapmanauthor.co.uk*

LINDA CHAPMAN

Sky Horses

Cloud Magic

Illustrated by Ann Kronheimer

PUFFIN

PUFFIN BOOKS

Published by the Penguin Group
Penguin Books Ltd, 80 Strand, London WC2R ORL, England
Penguin Group (USA) Inc., 375 Hudson Street, New York, New York 10014, USA
Penguin Group (Canada), 90 Eglinton Avenue East, Suite 700, Toronto, Ontario, Canada M4P 2Y3
(a division of Pearson Penguin Canada Inc.)
Penguin Ireland, 25 St Stephen's Green, Dublin 2, Ireland (a division of Penguin Books Ltd)
Penguin Group (Australia), 250 Camberwell Road, Camberwell, Victoria 3124, Australia
(a division of Pearson Australia Group Pty Ltd)
Penguin Books India Pvt Ltd, 11 Community Centre, Panchsheel Park, New Delhi – 110 017, India
Penguin Group (NZ), 67 Apollo Drive, Rosedale, North Shore 0632, New Zealand
(a division of Pearson New Zealand Ltd)
Penguin Books (South Africa) (Pty) Ltd, 24 Sturdee Avenue, Rosebank,
Johannesburg 2196, South Africa

Penguin Books Ltd, Registered Offices: 80 Strand, London WC2R ORL, England

puffinbooks.com

First published 2009
3

Text copyright © Linda Chapman, 2009
Illustrations copyright © Ann Kronheimer, 2009
All rights reserved

The moral right of the author and illustrator has been asserted

Set in Bembo 15/22pt
Typeset by Palimpsest Book Production Limited, Grangemouth, Stirlingshire
Made and printed in England by Clays Ltd, St Ives plc

British Library Cataloguing in Publication Data
A CIP catalogue record for this book is available from the British Library

ISBN: 978-0-141-32330-5

www.greenpenguin.co.uk

Penguin Books is committed to a sustainable future
for our business, our readers and our planet.
The book in your hands is made from paper
certified by the Forest Stewardship Council.

*To the four grey horses and
ponies who lit up my life*

High
Above . . .

The snow-white stallion raised his head.
His ears flickered. Something was
wrong, but what? Tor's dark eyes swept
over the jagged mountains, deep valleys
and the meadows and streams of his
cloud kingdom, searching for something
that looked out of place. But his herd
was peaceful. The mares were grazing,
lifting their heads every so often to
check on the foals, who were chasing
each other nearby. Further off a group

of six young stallions were play fighting,
testing their strength. Tor's nostrils flared.
Everything looked normal. Down below
he knew that the people who lived on
the coast would be seeing white clouds
floating slowly across a calm sky. So
what was bothering him? Tor could feel
his eyes being drawn to a wood nearby.
Just outside it there was a large cloud
with a hole in the centre. Tor hesitated.
Could it be that? It had been seven
years since anyone had used it . . .

He tossed his head and trotted towards it.

One of the foals broke away from the others and galloped over. A beautiful pale grey, he was only young – his legs long and gangly, his short mane sticking up – but already his neck had the same proud arch as the stallion's.

'Mistral!' The stallion stopped to greet his son.

'Is everything all right, Father?' the foal asked.

'Yes,' Tor reassured him, nuzzling him gently. 'Everything is fine.'

'Where are you going?' Mistral asked eagerly. 'Can I come with you?'

Tor hesitated. But just then there was a soft whinny and he looked round to see Snowdance, his lead mare and

Mistral's mother, cantering over, her long mane sweeping almost to the ground. 'Stop bothering your father, Mistral,' she told the colt. 'Go back to your friends and play.'

Mistral looked as if he was about to argue, but his mother flattened her ears slightly and he gave in. Plunging round, he cantered back to the group of foals, kicking his heels up defiantly as he went.

Snowdance smiled as she watched him go and then she stepped towards Tor. They touched muzzles. His eyes searched her beautiful face. He could see she looked troubled.

'Do you feel it too?' he asked quietly.

Snowdance nodded. 'There is something in the air that feels wrong.'

He glanced towards the strange cloud formation by the trees and she followed his gaze.

'Perhaps someone is trying to speak to us again.'

'It does not feel quite like that . . . but maybe.'

Tor felt almost as if he was being pulled, urged closer. 'I will go to the gateway and see.'

They touched noses again and Tor plunged away. He cantered across the meadow towards the trees, his mane and tail streaming behind him. Anyone watching from below would have seen the clouds begin to move a little faster across the sky.

But what no one saw, not even Tor, was that in the shadow of the trees a dark figure waited . . .

CHAPTER

One

Erin walked down the lane, the wind catching at her long dark-blonde hair. Breathing in the sharp smell of seaweed, she looked longingly towards the path that led over the cliff top. 'Can I go down to the beach, Jo?' she asked.

Her stepmum, Jo, nodded. 'Of course. Just come and say a quick hello to Aunt Alice first. You know how much she likes to see you.'

Jo headed towards the small stone

cottage at the side of the lane. Overhead the seagulls cried out with high-pitched shrieks as they swooped across the cloudy sky, buffeted by the breeze. Glancing up at them, Erin thought how wonderful it would be to be a bird and be able to fly like that.

Black-headed gull, kittiwake, common gull . . . she thought, recognizing the different types of gull. She loved all animals and birds and wanted to be a vet when she was older – either that or a riding instructor. Horses were her favourite animals of all.

Jo glanced over her shoulder. 'Come on, Dizzy Daydreamer!'

Erin sighed. She was always getting teased by her family for daydreaming. Jo, her dad and her three older stepbrothers were all really loud and sporty and thought she was odd because she was quiet and liked reading. Erin loved books, particularly ones about magic, although now she was eleven she didn't dare admit that she still believed in magic because she knew how much she would be teased at school and at home. No one understood.

If only I had a proper best friend, she thought, *someone who loves the same things as me*. But she didn't. Her two best friends had once been Fran and Katie who she sat with at school and also went riding with, but ever since they'd found out they were going to a different secondary school from her in September they had been going off together and whispering behind her back.

She tried not to think about them as she ran to join Jo at the cottage door. Jo's great-aunt opened it. She was slightly stooped with short grey hair.

'Hello, dear,' Aunt Alice said, moving forward stiffly to kiss Jo on the cheek. 'And Erin too,' she said, her cloudy blue eyes lighting up. 'How lovely to see you. Come in, both of you. Come in.'

As Erin and Jo went inside, Aunt Alice's two cats, Sooty and Muffin, padded over and started winding round Erin's legs. Erin crouched down and tickled their heads. 'Hi, boys.' They both purred and pressed their heads against her fingers. She picked Sooty up and gave him a cuddle.

'Now let me guess,' Aunt Alice said. 'It's not raining at the moment, Erin, so

I imagine you'll be wanting to go to the beach.'

Erin smiled and nodded. Aunt Alice knew how much she loved going to the beach on her own.

'Off you run then, dear. We can catch up later.' Kissing Sooty's head, Erin put him down.

'Come back if it starts looking like it's going to rain again,' Jo said. She turned to Aunt Alice. 'I can hardly believe the weather we've had recently. It's so changeable. Storms one minute, bright sunshine the next. I've never known anything like it.'

'There was weather like this once years ago when I was about four,' said Aunt Alice. 'We had days of wild storms followed by days of burning sun. It ended in the great storm of 1923. I've told you about that, haven't I, Erin?'

Erin nodded and shivered as she remembered Aunt Alice's story of the enormous storm. The sea had flooded the villages on the coast, the rivers had burst their banks, houses had been wrecked and lots of people and animals had died.

'I remember learning about the Great Storm when I was at school,' Jo commented. 'Can you imagine how dreadful it would be if something like that happened again?'

Leaving the grown-ups to discuss the weather, Erin slipped back outside.

The weather had changed again already, the wind dying down to just a gentle breeze. Patches of blue sky, the same colour as Erin's eyes, were showing through the clouds overhead. It was weird what the weather was doing at the moment. *Maybe it's something to do with global warming*, Erin thought, remembering what they had been learning about the term before.

She ran down the lane and took the footpath at the end that led between high hedges towards the sea. Happiness bubbled through her as she let her mind fill with thoughts of horses. What horse would she have if she could have any in the world? A black stallion with a white star? A chestnut show-jumping pony? A dapple-grey Arab pony? Yes. That's what she would choose.

Imagining she was riding him, Erin held her hands as if she was holding reins, clicked her tongue and cantered forward, changing legs every few strides. 'There's a good boy,' she said. She shied, pretending he had seen something in the hedge that had spooked him, and cantered on round the corner to where the footpath opened out on to the cliff top.

Erin stopped, her cheeks flushing as she saw a woman and two girls about her age walking towards her on the cliff path. The woman, who had long wavy blonde hair, smiled at her. 'Hello.'

The girls also grinned in a friendly way. One looked as if she might be the

14

woman's daughter. She had blonde corkscrew curls and a mischievous face. The other girl had lively hazel eyes and skin the colour of milk chocolate. Her hair was a thick mass of dark brown ringlets that reached her shoulders.

Erin groaned inside. How embarrassing! They must have seen her pretending to ride a horse. 'Hi,' she muttered, her cheeks burning. She hurried on past them.

'Come on, Allegra!' she heard the dark-haired girl call as the three of them passed her, turning down the footpath. 'Race you back to the village!'

Erin ran on along the cliff top, glad to leave them behind and be on her own again. The sea was on her left, the waves dragging on the pebbles of the strip of stony beach. On her right there was a patchwork of green and yellow fields divided by grey stone walls and hedges bursting with the white hawthorn flowers that always bloomed in May. In several of the fields were horses and ponies.

Erin stopped to stroke one pony who had his face over the fence, but the grumpy local farmer was in the field and he shouted at her. Erin hurried on her way.

Daydreaming about the ponies she would have if she lived in a farmhouse with a stable block and fields of her own, Erin turned on to a path half hidden by overgrown bushes and small trees. It led down to the beach. The stones were rough beneath her feet and the path was so steep in places she had to hang on to tufts of grass, but she had been down it so often she knew exactly where she had to be careful.

She reached the small beach and walked along it a little way before sitting down on a large dry rock. This was one of her favourite places in the world. It was very quiet apart from the

birds, completely different from the busy touristy beach down the coast where her stepbrothers loved to hang out.

Her eyes followed the jagged headland round. At the furthest tip there was a spit of land that ended in three enormous stones. They jutted up out of the sea, two standing upright and a round one that looked like an enormous Polo. The hole in it was so large that an adult could easily climb through it. The three rocks were known locally as World's End. It was just about possible to walk to them from the beach, but if the tide was high the spit of land got covered up.

Erin moved her toes in the stones. They tumbled over each other, grey, white and brown. Her gaze searched across them. Could she see any hagstones? They were stones with holes in the middle, like miniature versions of the round World's End stone.

Aunt Alice had told her that in the old days people used to hang hagstones up outside the houses to keep witches away and that they had tried to do magic with them. She'd said that people used to believe that they could be used for working weather magic or healing magic or casting spells of protection. *Witchstones*, they were called then. Erin had always been very good at finding them.

There! she thought, suddenly spotting one.

It was a round, grey stone with lines

of white shot through it. She picked it up. In the centre there was one circular hole, big enough for her to fit a finger through. Erin turned the stone over in her hand. It was cold and smooth. Sometimes hagstones had lots of holes, sometimes they had a hole on one side that hadn't gone through to the other side completely and sometimes there was a small hole blocked by a chip of rock or shell. They were all different. She kept the best ones for her collection at home.

Erin studied the stone carefully.

She liked the way the grey and white streaked together and the smoothness of the sides. She would definitely keep this one. As she held it, the rattle of the stones on the beach seemed to grow slightly louder.

What would it be like if hagstones really could be used for working magic like people used to believe? she thought. *Wouldn't that be amazing?*

Lifting the stone up so that it was pointing at the clouds she looked idly through the hole.

Erin almost dropped the stone in shock. *Horses!* There were grey horses in the sky! Some were cantering, some walking, others were standing in groups

in a cloud land of hills and valleys,
streams and rivers . . .

Abruptly, she blinked and looked up
at the skies without the stone. The
clouds looked normal again. 'Weird,' she
muttered. Was it just her imagination?
She had often watched the sky and
imagined a cloud take on the shape of
a dragon or a castle or something else.
But something about this felt different.
It had been like looking at a film.
There had been loads of horses – a
whole land full of them. Erin stared at
the stone in her hand. It had been just
her imagination, hadn't it?

It can't be real, she told herself. *You
know it can't be*. Quickly, she lifted the
hagstone again, her heart thudding in
her chest.

She gasped as she watched a young grey colt rear up playfully at another and a group of older mares trot past in the clouds. There really *were* horses in the sky!

CHAPTER

TWO

Erin tore along the cliff. By the time
she reached the lane she had a stitch in
her side from running so fast, but she
didn't stop. She raced up to the cottage
and banged on the door.

Jo opened it. Taking one look at
Erin's wide eyes, she frowned. 'What is
it, Erin? Are you OK?'

'In the sky! I've seen something in
the sky!' Erin's lungs hurt as she
grabbed great mouthfuls of air.

'What are you talking about?' Jo said in astonishment.

Aunt Alice appeared in the lounge doorway. 'Is everything all right, Erin?'

'No,' said Erin, staring wildly at them both. 'There are horses in the sky!'

'Horses in the sky?' Jo's face visibly relaxed. 'Oh, Erin. You had me worried there for a moment. You and your imagination!'

'I'm not making it up. It's true!' Erin exclaimed. 'Look!' She thrust the hagstone into Jo's hand. 'Look at the clouds through that!'

Jo shook her head disbelievingly and lifted the stone up. As she looked through it, she gasped and clutched her heart. 'Yes! Horses!'

'You can see them too!' Erin

exclaimed in relief. She wasn't going mad after all!

'Yes, and a fire-breathing monster and a fairy.' Jo laughed and handed the stone back.

Erin felt the air rush out of her as if she was a balloon that had just been punctured. 'But there *are* horses there,' she said in confusion. 'I can see them.' She turned desperately to Aunt Alice. 'Can you see them, Aunt Alice?'

'Oh, Erin . . .' Jo started to frown.

But Aunt Alice came to the door, took the stone and looked through it. Erin held her breath, but the old lady shook her head. 'All I can see is clouds, my dear.' She looked thoughtfully at Erin. 'I do remember, though, that when I was little there was a story told about horses made of clouds – sky horses, they were called. People said their movements controlled the weather. If the horses were quiet, the clouds moved gently, but if they were restless there would be wind and rain, and if they fought that would bring great storms. It was rumoured that if you looked up on very stormy days you could sometimes see them. I looked and looked, but I never did see them even though I really wanted to.'

'Aunt Alice, don't encourage her!' exclaimed Jo. 'She's got a vivid enough imagination as it is.'

Erin took no notice. *Sky horses*, she thought. She looked up at the skies through the stone again. Even if Aunt Alice and Jo couldn't see them, she could – a herd of grey horses ranging in colour from the palest white to the darkest steel grey, tossing their manes, trotting together, wheeling round and breaking into a canter as more and more clouds covered the skies.

Aunt Alice squeezed Erin's arm. 'Would you like a biscuit and a drink?'

Erin hesitated, but she could tell there was no point saying anything more about the sky horses to Aunt Alice and Jo. They would not believe her. *It's just me*, she thought. *Maybe I'm going mad. Unless . . . unless it's* magic!

The word rang out in her head. Her mind whirled.

Please let it be magic, she thought.

Later that afternoon, Jo and Erin walked back to their house in the village. As they walked in through the front door, Jake, Erin's twelve-year-old brother, came charging down the stairs with a ball under his arm.

'Goal!' he yelled, shooting the ball over the banisters so that it almost knocked Erin's head off. It bounced on to the floor and crashed into a table.

Ben and Sam, who were fourteen and fifteen, hurried through from the kitchen to the lounge where the telly was blaring out a football match. 'It's going to be two–one,' Ben was saying.

'Nah, I reckon it's going to be three all and go to penalties,' said Sam.

'Hi, boys,' Jo said wryly. 'Nice to see you too.'

Erin hurried up to her bedroom and closed the door, shutting out the sound

of the TV and the voices. Her room
was small, just big enough for a bed, a
wardrobe and a desk. But it had a
window at the end with a wide sill.
There was an old dark wooden box on
it filled with hagstones. It had once
belonged to her mum. Not Jo, her
stepmum, but her real mum, who had
died when Erin was three. Erin had
always liked to play with the stones.

Sitting down on the windowsill, Erin
pulled the box towards her. Putting the
hagstone she had found at the beach
down beside her, she nervously picked
up another stone from the box. Would
she still see the horses with a different
stone?

She held it to the skies. There they
were! The clouds were grey and thick,

jagged in places like mountain ranges.
There were mares with young foals,
older horses, a group of young stallions.
She had never seen such beautiful horses.
They had manes and tails that swept to
the floor, large dark eyes, delicate legs
and arched necks. They were just as she
had always imagined unicorns would be,
but without the horns.

'Weather weaver!' A commanding
voice suddenly seemed to echo into her
mind. Erin swung round. It sounded

like someone was speaking just behind her, but there was nobody there.

'W–what . . . w–who . . .?' Erin stammered, looking around her bedroom wildly. 'What . . .?'

'Do not be scared. I am a sky stallion.' The voice was strong but gentle at the same time. 'The hagstone you are holding lets you hear me in your thoughts. Only weather weavers can do this.'

Erin's head spun. 'A . . . a weather weaver! What's that?'

'*You* are a weather weaver, child. You have just never realized it before. What is your name?'

'Erin. What . . . who are you?'

'My name is Tor. I usually lead the herd you have seen in the skies. We control the weather through our movements. Sometimes we bring rain, sometimes wind, sometimes clear days. But now a dark one has come who seeks to take control of the weather so that all shall live in fear. The dark one has trapped me here on Earth using magic. Without me, my sky herd is restless. If I do not return soon, I fear that fighting will break out and that the weather will descend into chaos, bringing storms and devastation to this land.'

Erin shivered as she remembered Aunt Alice's story about the last great storm.

'Erin,' Tor's voice interrupted her thoughts. 'I need your help.'

Erin blinked. 'My help? But what can I do?'

'You must use the power you have as a weather weaver to –' Tor broke off. 'The dark one comes!' He whinnied fiercely and then suddenly there was silence.

'H-hello?' Erin said quickly. 'Are you there? Tor?'

There was no reply.

Erin felt totally bewildered. The words that she had just heard echoed around her head: *my sky herd is restless . . . the weather will descend into chaos . . . you must use the power you have . . .*

She held the stone tightly. Maybe the stallion would talk some more. She desperately wanted to know how she could help him.

'Hello?' she said. 'Tor?'

But nothing happened.

'Erin! We're all going down to the beach. Get your things,' her dad called up the stairs.

Erin stood up shakily and went to the door. She didn't want to go in case Tor tried to talk to her again. She had to find out more. 'Can't I stay here, Dad?' she asked, looking out and feeling very strange.

Her dad shook his head. 'Sorry, sweetheart. You're not old enough to stay home on your own. You know that.'

Erin knew there was no point arguing. She fetched a book and, putting the hagstone into her pocket, she went downstairs and got into the car with her brothers. Their village was only a short drive away from a busy sandy beach just along the coast. While

her dad and her brothers played football on the sand, Erin found a quiet place near the edge of the sand dunes and opened her book, but she ended up not reading a word. Her thoughts were too full of what had happened.

Magic really existed! She could hardly believe it, but it did. A sky stallion – a horse made up of actual clouds – had spoken to her and told her she was something called a weather weaver. Erin was tempted to look at the clouds again through the hagstone, but she knew if her brothers or dad noticed they would ask her what she was doing and think she was strange.

The skies were grey. She rubbed the goosebumps on her bare arms, not knowing whether to feel excited or alarmed. She really wished she could share it with someone. But who? Not Fran and Katie, that was for sure. They would just laugh at her. And Dad, Jo and her brothers were out of the question. They already thought she had an overactive imagination. They'd never believe her! *Oh, if only I had someone I could talk to*, she thought longingly.

She remembered what Tor had said about how a storm would come if he didn't return to the skies soon. What if it was a really big storm like the one Aunt Alice remembered? What if it was so bad that people were killed again? Erin looked at her brothers and her dad. She couldn't bear it if anything happened to them – to anyone. She had to help stop it if she could. But she didn't have the faintest idea what she could do

Just then her dad left the others and came jogging up the beach towards her. 'Hey, Erin!' he called. 'We're going to go and get something to eat at the café. Do you want to come too?'

'Yep.' Erin got slowly to her feet.

Her dad looked at her worried face. 'Are you OK, sweetheart?' he asked in concern. 'You don't look very happy.'

'I'm fine,' Erin said quickly. 'It's just . . . just a sad bit in my book.'

'You need cheering up then,' her dad said. 'How does a hot dog and chips followed by a banana split sound?'

Erin forced a smile. 'It sounds great, Dad. Thanks.'

And, trying to push thoughts of the hagstone and the sky stallion into the back of her mind for now, she followed her dad towards the bright and bustling café.

CHAPTER

Three

Before Erin went to bed that night, she
went over to the wooden box on her
windowsill and ran her fingers through
the smooth hagstones, searching for
something buried deep inside them.
Her fingers found the scrap of paper
that her mum had always kept in the
box with the stones.

She took it out. It was old and the
writing had faded. At some point in
time someone had spilt some water or a

drink on the bottom half of the page
and the ink there had washed
completely away leaving only a few
faint marks. The bits she could read
sounded almost like a poem. She knew
it well.

When the dark one returns, the door
  shall be reopened
And danger will threaten all living
  below.
If the binding is broken, they can be
  protected,
But one coming willingly lets the dark's
  power grow.
Until . . .

And that was it. The rest of the words
had been washed away.

She reread the first line again. *The dark one*. The words had been niggling at her. Just before Tor had stopped speaking to her she was sure he had said: 'The dark one is here.'

Erin shivered. Was it just coincidence? *Oh, Tor*, she thought longingly, *speak to me again*.

She got into bed. Exhausted by everything that had happened that day, she soon fell asleep, her hand holding the hagstone. She didn't know how long she had been asleep, but some time later she was aware of a voice in her head.

'Weather weaver!'

'Tor! Is that you?' she said, not knowing if she was dreaming or awake.

'Yes. Come and find me near World's

End,' he said urgently. 'Search for the black weathervane of a rearing horse. You will find me close by. I need your magic to return to the skies and stop the storms.'

'But what magic?' Erin asked, confused.

'Your weather-weaving magic. You have many powers, Erin, that you do not know about yet, but to learn about them you must first discover your stardust form.'

'W-what's that?' Erin stammered in confusion.

Tor broke off with a squeal and there was silence.

Erin suddenly found herself blinking her eyes open. She realized she was in her silent bedroom, lying in her bed in the dark. Clutching the stone, she sat up.

She swallowed. She was sure the stallion speaking to her hadn't been a dream. She thought about what Tor had said. She didn't know anything of the 'stardust' he had mentioned, but World's End – she knew that.

Almost before realizing what she was doing, Erin jumped out of bed. She was filled with an irresistible urge to go to World's End. Glancing at her clock, she saw it was well past midnight. The house was quiet. Everyone must be asleep. Pulling on her jeans and T-shirt, she left the room. She knew she shouldn't go, but something was pushing her on. She tiptoed down the stairs and let herself out of the back door.

Seconds later, Erin was running down the deserted street. Her heart pounded in her chest so hard she could hardly breathe. She knew that if Jo and her dad found out she was outside the house in the middle of the night, she would be in real trouble. She would never have gone out on her own normally, but all she could think about was going to World's End and seeing if she could find Tor. Erin's imagination overflowed with the magic and adventure of it all. She ran down the lane past Aunt Alice's house. *I have to go to World's End. He's near there. If I find him, he'll be able to tell me more and tell me what I can do to help.*

The moon was full and lit her way across the cliff top. She scrambled and slipped down the path to the beach near World's End where she had first seen the horses among the clouds. Reaching it, she paused and looked around at the waves moving in and out, pulling at the shingle. What should she do now? She didn't know. She took a deep breath. Suddenly she felt very alone, out there in the starlit night.

'*Tag!*'

Erin jumped as a girl's voice came out of the sky.

'Got you!'

'No, you didn't!'

'Yes, I did!'

Erin looked around wildly. There was
no one there.

'No, you didn't!'

Erin gasped as suddenly two girls,
both her age, appeared out of thin air,
flying in the starry sky. 'B-but –
b-but . . .' she stammered.

At the sound of her voice the girls

looked down. They both looked
horrified.

'*Camouflagus!*' Erin heard them say,
and they both vanished instantly.

'Wait!' Erin shouted. 'Who are you?
Come back!' Hope surged through her.
She didn't know who they were, but
they *must* be magic. Maybe they could
help her? 'Please! Do you know
anything about sky horses? About
weather weaving? Come back. I really
need your help!'

The air shimmered and one of the
girls appeared. She had blonde
corkscrew curls and was wearing a silver
dress. Erin frowned. She looked oddly
familiar.

'Allegra!' a voice exclaimed and then
the other girl appeared. She had dark

wavy hair and was wearing a golden dress.

Erin suddenly recognized them. It was the two girls she had seen on the cliff path that day. 'What . . . what's happening?' she whispered. 'Who are you? Are . . . are you . . .' she stared at them and said the only thing she could think of: '. . . *fairies?*'

The blonde girl smiled. 'Don't be silly.' She flew down and landed lightly on the shingle beside her. 'We're stardust spirits, of course!'

Four

Erin stared at the blonde girl. 'Stardust spirits?'

'Yes, but you must be one too if you've heard about sky horses and weather weaving,' said the blonde girl. 'I'm Allegra, by the way. And this is Chloe,' she added as the dark-haired girl landed next to her on the beach.

'Hi,' Chloe said easily. 'Who are you?'

'My name's Erin.' Erin shrugged helplessly.

'What do you know about weather weaving?' Allegra asked.

'Nothing apart from the fact I think I might be a weather weaver.' Erin saw their astonished looks. 'It's a long story.'

'Tell us,' urged Allegra.

So Erin took a deep breath and told them about discovering she was a weather weaver and everything that had happened to her that day, including the sky stallion speaking to her and telling her he was trapped.

'Wow!' said Chloe as Erin finished. 'That sounds so cool! I've never even heard of sky horses.'

'I have though. It's because Chloe's only been a stardust spirit for two days,' Allegra quickly explained. 'But I've been a stardust spirit for ages. Xanthe, my mum, is one too. When we saw you at the beach today, she said she thought you looked like you might have stardust powers. She's really good at recognizing people who have. She was right this time!'

Allegra seemed to see the bewilderment on Erin's face. 'Do you want to sit down and I'll tell you all about stardust?'

Erin nodded and they sat down together on the large rocks at the bottom of the cliff. The stone felt reassuringly solid beneath Erin's legs. She felt almost as if she was in a dream. She believed in magic, but this was all so weird!

'Being a stardust spirit is brilliant!' Chloe burst out before Allegra could begin. 'You can fly and do magic!'

Allegra grinned. 'Every person in the
world has stardust inside them – it's
what makes humans imaginative and
creative. But some people have extra
stardust and these people can turn into
stardust spirits at night time.'

'We have to help nature – using our
magic to put right any wrongs done by
people,' Chloe added.

'And you're saying I am a stardust
spirit,' said Erin slowly.

Allegra nodded. 'Weather weavers are a
special kind of stardust spirit. It's very

unusual to be a weather weaver though –
they can talk to the sky horses like you
can and do magic with hagstones. I don't
know much more about them because
I've never met one before. I bet Xanthe
would love to meet you. She's not with
us tonight because she had some other
stardust spirits to see; everyone is really
worried about the strange weather that's
been happening and it sounds like you've
found out the reason for it all. Xanthe
and I go home to Devon tomorrow –
we've been staying at Chloe's house for
the last few days . . .'

'Xanthe's my godmother as well as
being Allegra's mum,' Chloe put in.
'She and Allegra told me about stardust
two nights ago. They made it sound
as if it was a story, but as soon as I

heard about it I had to try and turn into a stardust spirit to see if it was real.'

'So how do I become a stardust spirit?' Erin asked anxiously. 'I don't know how to be like you — how to fly!'

Allegra rose into the air, her green eyes twinkling as she looked down at Erin. 'You need to stand in the starlight and say "I believe in stardust" three times,' she instructed. 'The first time you do it the stars have to be in the right place otherwise it won't work, but they are at the moment.'

'You've got to really, really mean the words as you say them,' warned Chloe.

That part was easy for Erin. After all the magic that had happened and having seen Allegra and Chloe flying in the sky,

Erin had no doubt that stardust was real.

She took a deep breath. 'I believe in stardust. I believe in stardust. I believe in stardust!'

As Erin said the words for the third time, all the weight seemed to drain out of her body and she suddenly shot up into the air. She cried out, realizing that her jeans and T-shirt had changed into a sparkling pale-blue dress, the colour of a clear winter sky. 'Oh wow!' she exclaimed.

Allegra and Chloe quickly flew up to join her and took her hands.

'How does it feel?' Chloe grinned at her.

'Amazing!' breathed Erin, looking around her.

'Oh, this is so exciting!' Chloe twirled round in the air. 'I was dreading Allegra and Xanthe going home because Xanthe thought there weren't any other stardust spirits who lived near here, but now there's you! We can go flying together and meet up every night – if you want to, of course?'

'Oh yes!' Erin said eagerly. 'I'd love to!' Normally she was shy when she first met people, but she didn't feel shy with Chloe and Allegra at all.

'We'll show you how to fly!' said Allegra. She and Chloe guided Erin around the sky, showing her how to go up and down, turn round, spin in circles and camouflage herself so no one could see her and it appeared as if she had vanished into the sky. Allegra then left her with Chloe on the beach and darted around, showing how it was possible to do steep dives, somersaults and pirouettes.

'You're so good at flying, Allegra!' Chloe said enviously.

'You'll both be this good soon,' said Allegra, shrugging. 'It just takes practice.'

Chloe grinned at Erin. 'We can practise lots together.' She frowned suddenly. 'Allegra! Why has Erin got a blue dress? I

thought you told me all stardust spirits
had pearly-grey clothes when they first
became stardust spirits, like I did, and then
their clothes change when they realize
what type of spirit they are.'

'Well, I'm not completely sure,' said
Allegra, flying down and looking at
Erin's sparkling dress. 'But I guess it's
probably something to do with the fact
that all weather weavers are winter spirits,
so right from the start if you know
you're a weather weaver then you know
what type of spirit you are and don't
have to find out like normal spirits do.'

'What are you talking about?' Erin
asked, looking from Allegra to Chloe in
confusion.

'Oh, there's so much for you to
learn!' Allegra smiled. 'There are four

different types of stardust spirit – spring, summer, autumn and winter. They each wear different-coloured clothes and can do different types of magic.'

'Summer spirits like me wear gold and can make things heat up,' said Chloe proudly.

'I'm an autumn spirit and we wear silver and can make the wind blow,' said Allegra, smoothing down the skirt of her silver dress. 'Spring spirits wear green and can make things grow, and winter spirits wear blue, although it's usually a darker blue than your dress, and they can make it rain, snow or hail.'

Erin's head spun. 'So I'll be able to do that as well as controlling the weather?'

'Well, you *will* be able to one day,' said Allegra. 'Doing magic properly

usually takes quite a lot of practice.'

A shiver ran down Erin's spine. 'But I might not have time to practise. I have to find the stallion and help him get back to the sky so he can stop storms from coming.'

Allegra bit her lip. 'I really wish Xanthe was here now. I wonder who has trapped the stallion. It might have been a dark spirit.' She shuddered.

'What's a dark spirit?' Erin asked nervously.

'A male or female stardust spirit who's turned bad,' Allegra explained. 'They want more and more power and magic, and will do anything to have it. If a dark spirit trapped a sky stallion they would be able to have complete control over the weather.' She saw the alarm on Erin's face. 'Look, don't worry. I'll tell Xanthe all about this and then we'll email Chloe and tell you what you should do.'

'Thanks,' Erin said in relief. It was good to know she wasn't going to have to figure things out on her own any more. She knew she should probably go back soon. She really didn't want to after such an amazing night, but if her parents found she was gone, and there was no note or anything, they'd be worried sick. 'I should go home now,' she said reluctantly.

'Maybe you and I could meet tomorrow and start looking for the stallion,' said Chloe eagerly. 'We could try to find this place with a black weather-vane he told you about. We don't have to be stardust spirits to look. We could start searching in the day. Why don't we meet here in the morning?'

'I can't in the morning – I'm going riding,' said Erin. 'But I could meet up in the afternoon. I've not seen you around; do you live in Long Medlow?'

'Yes, but we only moved here two weeks ago,' Chloe explained. 'We're just outside the village. It's an old chapel. It's been turned into a house. Oh, I'm so glad I've met you. I haven't made any proper friends since I got here. I've started going to St Anne's School, but everyone in my class has already got a best friend.'

'It's like that in my class too,' sighed Erin. She suddenly wanted to tell Chloe all about Fran and Katie, but realized she really needed to go now. She could tell her tomorrow. 'I'll meet you here at about two o'clock then?'

Chloe nodded.

Allegra hugged Erin. 'Xanthe and I will mail you at Chloe's and we should be back visiting Chloe soon. We'll see you then. Good luck with finding the stallion.'

'Thanks,' Erin told her gratefully.

'Oh, and don't tell anyone that you're a stardust spirit,' Allegra warned her.

'You're only allowed to talk about it with other stardust spirits.'

'See you tomorrow,' Chloe called. 'When you get home, you need to say "Stardust be gone" and then you'll change back to normal. Otherwise you'll be a stardust spirit until the morning!'

'Thanks!' Erin said with a grin. 'See you tomorrow!'

Waving goodbye, she flew back towards her house. Her mind was buzzing with everything she had found out, but inside she felt ten times lighter. So much had happened that day, but at least she had friends she could talk with about it now.

I'm not on my own any more, she thought. Relief flowed through her as she practised swooping through the sky, the stars shining above her.

CHAPTER

Five

When Erin woke up, she thought for a
moment that the night before had just
been a dream. But it hadn't. She hugged
her knees to her chest in delight.

Sitting up in bed, she glanced towards
her window. The curtains were still
open and she could see that the sky
was covered with grey clouds. She got
out of bed and picked up one of the
hagstones from the box. The horses
were there. They were moving around

restlessly. The mares and foals were
huddled together. They looked unhappy.

*I've got to find Tor and set him free so he
can go back to them*, Erin thought.

She felt very glad as she remembered
that Chloe had suggested they meet
up that day. It would be so much better
searching for the sky stallion with a
friend rather than on her own.

Watching the horses in the clouds,
she wondered what the day would hold.

When Erin arrived at Hawthorn Stables
that morning, she went to the tack
room and found Fran and Katie there.
They were looking at a magazine.

'Hi,' Erin said to them.

'Hi,' Katie said briefly.

Fran didn't say anything. She was

short and slim and had shoulder-length blonde hair. Katie was much taller with brown hair tied back in a ponytail.

'What are you reading?' Erin asked them.

'Just *Pony* magazine,' said Fran. She closed it pointedly as Erin tried to look at it. 'Have you seen who you're riding today?' There was a smirk on her face.

'No,' Erin replied.

'Wilf.' Fran and Katie looked at each other and giggled. Wilf was the oldest pony on the yard and he was really slow and lazy.

Erin felt a flash of disappointment. They were going on a beach ride and she'd been hoping to ride one of the faster ponies. *Oh well*, she thought quickly, *never mind*. She pictured Wilf's cute face: he had a big stripe down his nose and gorgeous big brown eyes. He might not be the fastest pony, but she still loved him just like she loved all of the ponies.

'I'm riding Misty,' said Katie happily.

'And I'm riding Tango,' said Fran. She gave Erin a mean look. 'Shame you're just on slow, old Wilf, Erin. I bet you won't get him to go faster than a trot!'

Erin would usually have been starting

to get upset by now – it hurt being
teased like that by girls who used to be
her friends – but she had so much else
on her mind that she suddenly found
she couldn't be bothered to be upset by
Fran and Katie. If they only knew what
had been happening to her, they would
be so jealous!

'Never mind. I like Wilf,' she said,
shrugging and taking Wilf's head collar
from the hook. 'See you later.'

Erin had been riding at Hawthorn
Stables for five years. Now that she was
eleven, she helped out with the ponies
at the weekends and in the holidays.
There were quite a few girls who did
and Jackie, who owned the stables,
always tried to make sure they had

some free rides in return for all their
work. That day, because it was the half-
term holiday, Jackie had arranged a
beach ride for all the helpers. It was
great fun and Erin had a lovely time
riding Wilf. Being on the beach seemed
to give him a new burst of energy. He
galloped along the sands with all the
other ponies, and afterwards tossed his
head and snorted as they rode back.
She had the feeling he had really
enjoyed himself, and she had too.
She'd noticed that both Fran and Katie
had been struggling to control Tango
and Misty, who were younger and
livelier and who seemed to want to
shy and jog all the way there and back.
Erin patted Wilf, feeling very happy.
She wondered if Chloe liked horses.

Maybe they could go riding together if she did. That would be so much fun!

Excitement prickled through Erin as she thought about the afternoon. She really hoped they would find this place with the black weathervane, and find Tor. She wondered what he would look like. And what would he want her to do if she did find him? It felt so important to her already that she could use her new magic powers to help him.

I'll free him, she thought. *I'll help him get back to the sky.*

At two o'clock, Erin raced along the path that led to the beach, jumping over the puddles on the way. As she turned the corner on to the cliff top, she saw Chloe just ahead of her. 'Chloe!' she shouted. 'Wait!'

Chloe swung round. For a moment Erin felt shy. The other girl looked so different in her everyday clothes – green shorts and a T-shirt – would she still be as friendly as she had been the night before?

She needn't have worried. Chloe ran to meet her, her hazel eyes shining. 'Hi, Erin! I was so excited after we met last night! It's brilliant that you're a stardust spirit too and we can be friends, isn't it?'

Erin nodded eagerly. 'Oh yes.'

'So you were riding this morning?' Chloe went on. 'Where do you go? I love ponies! I used to ride every week and help out at the stables I went to. Mum has promised she'll find another

riding stables near here for me now we've moved.'

'You should come to the stables I go to,' said Erin. 'It's called Hawthorn Stables and it's only ten minutes away. Jackie, who owns it, is really nice and the ponies are lovely.'

'Brilliant! I'll ask Mum!' said Chloe. She lowered her voice. 'So, has Tor spoken to you again?'

Erin shook her head.

'What did he say exactly when he

spoke to you yesterday?' Chloe asked.

'That I would find him near the rocks at World's End and that I should look for a black weathervane that looked like a rearing horse.'

Chloe glanced around. 'Well, I guess we should get looking. Why don't we start with that house? That's the closest to World's End.' She pointed to the nearest house on the cliff top, an old grey stone farmhouse nestling in some fields with a small wood behind it.

'My gran used to own that house,' said Erin. 'It's called Lookout Point. It's had quite a few people living in it since my gran died. Someone new has just moved in. I've seen two horses in the fields by it, but I don't think it's got a black weathervane.'

'We should probably check it out just in case,' said Chloe. 'Come on!'

They headed towards the house. As they walked, they chatted about ponies and their families. They didn't stop until they reached the fields around Lookout Point. There were two horses there, a bay and a chestnut.

'Should we climb over the fence and go up to the house?' Chloe wondered.

Erin hesitated. 'There isn't a footpath.' She thought of the old farmer who had shouted at her the other day, and always told her off if she ever went into one of his fields without a footpath.

'We can't let that stop us!' said Chloe. 'Anyway, look.' She pointed to one of the horses. 'That bay horse's rug has slipped. If anyone tells us off for going into the field, we can just say we were trying to get to the house to let the owners know about it.'

Erin nodded. 'OK.' It was a good plan.

They climbed over the fence and headed towards the house. There was a gate between its stable yard and the field.

As they reached the gate, Chloe gasped. 'Look!' She grabbed Erin's arm.

Erin followed her gaze. On the roof of the stables behind the house was a black metal weathervane in the shape of a rearing horse!

Six

A black weathervane!

'The new owners must have put it up!' Erin whispered.

'The stallion *must* be somewhere near here,' Chloe said in a low voice. 'I wonder if the owners know about him. What shall we –' She broke off. A woman was coming towards them. She was tall and slim, wearing burgundy jodhpurs and a black T-shirt. Her long, dark-blonde hair, a similar colour to

Erin's, was held back in a low ponytail. She frowned slightly. 'This is private property,' she called.

'We just came over because there's a horse in this field whose New Zealand rug has slipped,' Chloe explained.

The frown faded immediately from the woman's face. 'Oh, right. I see. That's my horse, Gemini. Well, thanks for coming to tell me, girls. I'll go and fix it.'

She opened the gate and came into the field.

'Your horses are lovely,' called Chloe. 'Do you have any others?'

'No, just those two,' said the woman. 'Are you two girls local?'

'Yes, we both live in the village,' said Chloe chattily, joining her. 'We love horses. I'm Chloe and this is Erin, by the way.'

'Erin?' the woman turned. For a moment Erin thought she was going to ask her something, but she just smiled. 'That's an unusual name, Erin. Well, I'm Marianne. I've moved here fairly recently.'

'Would you like some help with your horses?' Chloe asked hopefully as they walked across the field. 'We could groom or clean tack for you.'

'Thanks for the offer, Chloe, but I'd

better say no. I'm sure your parents wouldn't like you coming here without them knowing me,' said Marianne. 'I'll see you around, girls. Bye!' She walked swiftly away.

Chloe sighed as they wandered back down towards the cliffs. 'Oh, Erin, Tor has to be close to here. Did you see there was a wood behind the stables? Maybe he's in there somewhere.'

'I want to go back and look,' said Erin.

'Tonight,' Chloe told her. 'We'll turn into stardust spirits and go then.'

'Do you think Marianne knows about him?' asked Erin. A thought struck her. 'Maybe she could be the dark one.'

'Oh no,' said Chloe. 'She seems nice.

Can you imagine her being a dark stardust spirit and capturing a sky stallion?'

Erin agreed it did seem a bit ridiculous.

'I bet he's being hidden secretly near here by someone else,' said Chloe.

'But who?' wondered Erin.

Chloe lifted her chin. 'I don't know, but we'll find out!'

Now that there was nothing more they could do about looking for Tor, they decided to go to Chloe's house. Chloe's mum, Nicky, was delighted Chloe had made a friend and came round to Erin's house to meet Jo. They got on just as well as the girls. Jo told Nicky all about Hawthorn Stables and gave her Jackie's number.

'I'll ring as soon as I get home,' Nicky promised. 'I bet you'd love to go and help there, wouldn't you, Chloe?'

'Oh yes!' Chloe breathed. 'Will you ask if I can start tomorrow?'

Nicky smiled. 'OK.'

They all walked to the door of Erin's house, and as the adults said goodbye Chloe whispered in Erin's ear: 'I'll see you tonight!'

Erin grinned. 'Yes! See you then!'

'I believe in stardust, I believe in stardust,' Erin murmured as soon as the house was quiet. 'I believe in stardust!'

On the last word she flew into the air. She had placed a couple of pillows under the duvet in her bed so it looked

as if she was still asleep. She had left a
note telling her parents not to worry,
she'd be back very soon, just in case
they did come in and check under the
covers. She hoped they wouldn't!

Taking a last look around her
bedroom, she flew out through the
open window. Her stomach turned
over nervously. What if they were
caught? *We can camouflage ourselves*, she
reminded herself, remembering how the
night before Allegra and Chloe had
taught her how to vanish against the

night sky. Feeling a bit better, she flew on.

Chloe was waiting for her on the beach. 'Let's go straight to Lookout Point!'

The two girls whispered, '*Camouflagus*,' and set off.

Erin's heart beat faster as they flew towards the house. It was shrouded in darkness. As they landed outside the stables, a horse snorted.

Erin checked over the stable doors. The chestnut was lying down and the bay was dozing, one hind foot resting.

Between the stables and the woods there was a small stone barn. They went over to it. Chloe opened the door as quietly as she could. Inside there was a tidy, well-kept tack and feed room.

Metal feed bins lined one wall of the room and there were bridles and head collars and keys hanging on hooks on the wall.

Shutting the door, they flew round the back of the barn. 'Let's try the woods,' Chloe suggested.

Usually Erin would have felt really scared being in the woods at night, but now she was a stardust spirit she felt OK. It was strange, but as she flew among the trees she felt almost as if she belonged there. Her eyes scanned the area. Suddenly she spotted a small grey stone building in a clearing. She frowned as they got closer. There was something on the ground. An icy chill swept through her as she realized that it was a circle made of hagstones.

'Look at —' she started to say, but a whinny interrupted her. It came from the building. 'Tor!' Erin exclaimed, recognizing the sound instantly.

She let her camouflage drop and raced to the door of the hut, her fingers fumbling with the bolt. 'Tor! It's me, Erin! Is that you?'

'Yes!' the sky horse's familiar whinny rang out. 'Can you let me out, Erin?'

The door was bolted and there was a big metal lock holding the bolt shut.

'No, the door's locked,' Erin said desperately.

'And there aren't any windows,' said Chloe, looking around.

'Who is that?' asked Tor immediately.

'Chloe. She's my friend. Another stardust spirit.' Erin rattled the bolt. 'Oh, Tor. I can't get you out.' Tears of frustration sprang to her eyes. Her fingers curled on the rough wood. If only she could get to him.

'Can you find the keys?' he said.

'But where will they be? Who's got them? Who's captured you? Who's −'

'Erin!' Tor interrupted. 'Quick! You and Chloe must go! The dark one is coming. I can sense it!'

'But who is the dark one?' Chloe demanded.

'There's no time! Go!' Tor's voice was full of alarm.

Chloe grabbed Erin's arm. 'Come on,' she said quickly.

Erin didn't want to leave the stallion, but Chloe tugged her upwards. 'Erin, we have to go!'

'*Camouflagus!*' Erin whispered urgently. Chloe echoed it.

They were only just in time. As they flew upwards, a dark, shadowy figure wearing a hooded cloak came striding through the trees.

CHAPTER

Seven

The two girls flew as fast as they could back to the cliff top. 'That was so scary!' Chloe said as they landed and let their camouflage fade. 'Did you see that figure?'

'Yes.' Erin's thoughts raced, full of relief at having found Tor, but full of alarm and fear too. 'I wonder who it was?'

'We have to find out!' Chloe said. 'You'll have to ask Tor when he speaks to you next.' She shivered. 'Oh, it's so annoying we couldn't stay for longer! What should we do now then? I guess we'd probably better not go back until tomorrow.'

'No,' said Erin in frustration. What she really wanted to do was fly straight back there and talk to Tor some more – maybe rescue him. But he had told them to go. 'I suppose we could try using our stardust powers. It might be good to practise them in case we need to use them to rescue Tor.'

'Good idea,' Chloe said.

'Why don't you show me what to do?' Erin suggested.

'OK!' Chloe replied eagerly. She pointed her hand at a dry twig on the floor in front of them. 'Fire be with me!'

The branch started to smoulder, a

curl of smoke rising up from its surface.
Chloe frowned in concentration and
the twig burst into flames.

'Fire be gone!' she said quickly. The
fire slowly died.

'Wow!' breathed Erin. She was so
impressed she almost forgot about the
dark spirit.

Chloe turned to her. 'Xanthe said
that some summer spirits can't make
fire straight away, but she said I must be
quite a strong spirit.' She tucked her
hair back behind her ears. 'You have a
go now. Just concentrate really hard on
what you want to happen and you
should feel a sort of tingling. That's
magic flowing through you. Say "Rain
be with me" and see if it works.'

'OK.' Erin felt excited. She looked at

the skies. *I can do this. I have to − for Tor!* 'Rain be with me!' she whispered intently.

A tingling feeling spread through her body, building up and up until it exploded out of her fingers. She gasped as a small raincloud formed above them. Raindrops immediately started falling.

Chloe squealed and dashed out from underneath it.

'Rain be gone! Rain be gone!' Erin gasped. Nothing happened and the rain soaked her. 'Rain be gone!' she cried again. This time the raincloud slowly faded.

Erin looked down at her dress. She was dripping wet.

Chloe giggled. 'I think you need to practise a bit!'

Erin tried again, but this time the cloud that appeared pelted them both with hailstones!

'I'm not very good at this,' she said, feeling embarrassed as she made the hail cloud finally vanish.

'Don't be silly,' Chloe said. 'It's only your first night of trying. You wouldn't expect to be good first time. You'll get better.'

Erin felt grateful. Usually, if she couldn't do something at school or the stables, Fran and Katie laughed at her and made her feel stupid. Chloe was so much nicer.

They practised some more. Chloe seemed to get better, starting fires and putting them out more quickly, but Erin didn't feel she was improving at all. She kept drenching herself and her hail clouds became snow clouds and her snow clouds became drizzling rain.

'You'll get the hang of it soon,' Chloe kept saying.

They played a game of tag and then finally decided to go home. 'I'll see you tomorrow,' Erin said.

'Yeah, at the stables at ten,' said Chloe

happily. 'Bye!' She waved, and they both darted away.

Erin got to the stables early. She checked the board and saw that she was going to be riding Tango that day. Unfortunately, he was Fran's favourite pony and Erin could tell that Fran wasn't pleased she wasn't going to be riding him. When Erin went into the tack room to fetch Tango's head collar and a grooming kit, Fran gave her a very dirty look. She was sitting on the wooden chest where all the grooming kits were kept.

'I need to get a grooming kit. Can you move, please, Fran?' Erin asked politely.

Her heart sank as Fran shook her

head. 'Nope,' she said, inspecting her nails. 'I don't feel like it.'

Erin hesitated, shrinking inside. What could she do? She needed a grooming kit, but she couldn't exactly push Fran off the chest, could she?

To her relief, two of the other helpers, Anna and Jodie, came in, also looking for grooming kits. Fran shifted immediately and as the other girls got their grooming kits out Erin quickly did the same. As she straightened up, Fran smirked at her as if saying *You know I wouldn't have moved just for you.* Erin tried to ignore her.

She left the tack room and saw Chloe coming out of the office with Jackie.

'Hi!' Erin went over, feeling very pleased to see her.

'Chloe's new. She's riding Solomon today. Will you show her around, please, Erin?' Jackie asked.

'Of course I will,' Erin said.

Jackie went back into the office. Just then Fran and Katie came out of the tack room. Fran stopped when she saw Chloe with Erin.

'Who are you?' she demanded curiously.

'Chloe,' Chloe replied easily. 'What's your name?'

'Fran. And this is Katie.' Fran looked Chloe up and down. She obviously approved of her because she smiled. 'Has Jackie told you who you'll be riding then?'

'Yes. Solomon.'

'Cool. Well, come with Katie and me

and we'll show you which pony he is.'

Chloe glanced at Erin. 'Erin's supposed to be showing me.'

'We don't need four of us to catch him, Erin,' Fran said pointedly. 'You can stay here.' She tossed her head. 'Come on, Chloe.'

Chloe stopped. 'Actually, you're right. We don't need four of us, and since I'm friends with Erin already she can show me which pony he is, can't you, Erin?'

Erin felt a rush of relief. She nodded.

'Thanks for the offer though,' Chloe said to Fran.

Fran looked very put out. 'Fine! Be like that then!' she snapped. 'Come on, Katie.' They marched off together.

Chloe grinned. 'Whoops, I think I might have offended her!' She didn't

look at all bothered. Erin envied her.
'So, are they the so-called friends you've
told me about?'

'Yes,' Erin replied.

'Well, you know what? Now I've met
them I think you're better off without
them,' said Chloe. 'Now, come on, I
want to see all the ponies!'

By the end of the day it was hard to
believe Chloe had only just started at the
stables. She'd helped with all the jobs no
one liked much, like sweeping around
the muckheap, and she'd started a water
fight when they'd been cleaning tack.
She was a good rider too and had got
Solomon going really well in the lesson.

'I've had a brilliant day!' she said
happily as she and Erin sat on the fence

and waited for Chloe's mum to collect them. 'It's such a cool yard! The ponies are gorgeous, Jackie's a really good teacher and everyone seems really nice. Well, apart from Fran and Katie. I don't know why you were ever friends with them.'

'They didn't use to be as mean,' Erin said, feeling she should defend them a bit. 'They've just changed this year.'

Chloe grinned. 'Well, I'm glad they have because it means we can be friends.'

Just then a shiny silver Land Rover pulled into the car park.

'It's Marianne!' Erin said in surprise as the blonde woman stepped out of the car.

'I wonder what she's doing here . . .' said Chloe.

'I don't know. I've never seen her here before,' said Erin. Marianne walked across the car park and saw the two girls sitting on the fence. A look of recognition crossed her face. 'Hey, didn't I meet you yesterday? You came and told me that Gemini's rug was coming off?'

'Yep, that was us,' answered Chloe.

'Well, thanks for that.' Marianne smiled. 'Most people would have just walked on by. It was really nice of you. Now, do you know where I can find Jackie? I want to talk to her about having some dressage lessons.'

'She's in the office,' Erin said, suddenly feeling silly. After finding Tor so close to Marianne's house, she had felt a little wary of her arrival at the stables, but hearing Marianne speaking about Jackie and her horses, Erin was sure she couldn't possibly be behind Tor's capture. 'Shall I show you where the office is?' she offered.

'That's OK. I've been here a few times before. But thanks for the offer, Erin.'

Marianne walked away.

'OK. She is so *not* the dark spirit,' Chloe whispered.

Erin nodded. 'I know. It has to be someone else. But who?'

Chloe shrugged. 'I don't know many people who live around here.'

'There's the horrible farmer who

always shouts at me if I stroke his horse,' Erin said, wracking her brain. 'Maybe it's him. He lives quite close to Lookout Point. I bet he could get to the woods where Tor is being kept really easily.'

Chloe's eyes widened. 'Maybe it *is* him then! I know! Let's go back to Lookout Point tonight. If the dark spirit comes, we can spy on them to see who they are and where they keep the keys for the barn.'

A shiver ran through Erin as she thought about the hooded figure they had seen the night before. It was a good idea, but she didn't like the idea of spying on a dark spirit at all!

Erin tried to use the hagstone to talk to Tor after she had got home from the stables, but there was no answer from him. As soon as she could, she raced through the dark to meet Chloe.

'I emailed Allegra and Xanthe, and told them about last night and the shadowy figure and asked what we should do but I haven't heard from them yet,' said Chloe. 'So I guess we should just follow our plan and try to spy on the dark spirit.'

Erin gulped. 'OK.'

They camouflaged themselves and flew to the woods. As they swooped down through the trees, Erin felt Chloe grab her hand and only just stopped herself from gasping out loud.

A magnificent snow-white stallion was standing in the clearing. And facing him was the hooded figure!

Eight

The dark spirit and the stallion stared at each other tensely. Tor was about seventeen hands high with an arched neck and dark eyes ringed by grey shadows. Erin had never seen a more majestic-looking or beautiful horse in her life. Underneath his long mane there was a coal-black rope round his neck.

The dark spirit was standing near the hagstone circle. 'You will do as I command, sky stallion!' her voice rang out.

In response Tor reared up, his front hooves striking out. 'Never!'

'You will!' the dark spirit exclaimed. Erin frowned. The voice sounded familiar. Who was it? But the next second the thought flew out of her head as the dark spirit pointed her hand towards Tor, clenched her fingers into a fist and twisted her wrist sharply.

Tor gave a loud squeal of pain and rage.

Raw wounds appeared on his neck under the rope. It seemed to be burning into his skin. 'I *will* be in command of the skies!' the hooded figure hissed. 'Come into the circle, King of the Clouds.' She twisted her hand again. Erin felt Chloe move beside her and grabbed her. They couldn't do anything. Every bit of her wanted to help, but they had so little power. They would only end up being caught or worse, and that wouldn't help Tor at all.

Chloe stopped, her fingers gripping Erin's.

Tor reared up again and then plunged at the spirit. She jumped back into the circle with a cry. For a moment, Tor's eyes burned with defiance. 'I am a sky stallion! I will not be commanded!'

And, with that, he turned and walked back into the hut.

The dark spirit watched him go. Then she muttered something under her breath, strode to the door and slammed it shut. She thrust the bolt across and

locked it. She was trembling with rage.
As she swung round, her hood fell back.

Erin caught her breath, her insides
turning to ice.

It was Marianne!

Her long blonde hair fell around her
shoulders. She was wearing a pale-blue
dress under the cloak. *Just like mine*,
Erin thought.

Yanking the keys on a big red key ring out of the lock, Marianne strode away through the trees.

When she was out of sight, Erin let her camouflage fade. Chloe appeared too, her face shocked. 'I can't believe it's Marianne after all!'

Erin could hardly believe it either. She felt sick as she thought of how Tor had been hurt. 'Did you see what she was doing to Tor? Oh, Chloe, we have to help set him free as soon as possible.'

'Why didn't he just gallop away?' wondered Chloe. 'Why did he walk back into the hut? Why didn't he escape?'

Erin didn't know. She looked at the hut below them. 'Come on. Let's go and talk to him.'

They flew down.

'Tor,' Erin whispered through the door.

'Erin,' the stallion said immediately. 'I sensed you were watching. It was lucky the dark one did not sense you too.'

'She was so cruel to you,' said Erin in dismay. 'Oh, Tor.'

'What was she trying to get you to do?' Chloe demanded.

'Enter the circle of hagstones so she could use me to control the weather in the sky,' Tor replied.

'But why did you go back into the hut?' asked Erin. 'Why didn't you just escape?'

'I cannot.' The stallion's voice was heavy. 'The rope round my neck is a binding rope made with dark magic. She came to my cloud kingdom through a gateway that links my world and this. She hid there and then caught me with the rope. While it is round my neck, I cannot escape from her. She can always call me back and I will never return to Snowdance and Mistral, my lead mare and son. Sky horses of royal blood can be used by weather weavers on Earth to control the weather. But I will not obey her.' Tor's voice was grim. 'I will not be part of her wicked scheme to control the skies. For as long as I am earthbound, I will fight her.'

'How can we help?' asked Erin.

'I need you to use your magic to destroy the binding rope, Erin. But first you must find the hagstone that Marianne used to create it. It will have three hairs from her head twisted round

it, through the hole in the centre. Find it and bring it to me with a rope made of bindweed, long enough to make a circle for you to sit in it with me, then I will tell you the spell. It is difficult, dangerous magic that only a weather weaver can perform.'

Erin swallowed. Difficult and dangerous magic – how could she possibly do that? 'I'm . . . I'm not very good at doing magic. I can't even make it rain very well and I don't know how to do any weather-weaving magic at all,' she stammered.

'You know more than you think, child,' said Tor gently. 'Your powers are very special. It will not be easy, but I will help you and I believe you will be able to do it. Go now. It is not safe to stay. A storm is approaching. I can feel it and the dark one may return at any moment.'

'Is that why you sometimes can't speak to me,' Erin realized, 'because she is here?'

'Yes,' said Tor. 'But I will talk to you when I can. Now go!'

Erin and Chloe flew away. The wind was getting up, and overhead there was an ominous rumble of thunder.

'Tor was right. There *is* a storm coming!' said Chloe.

'We have to get him back to the skies,' said Erin.

'That's going to mean getting into Marianne's house to try to find the hagstone he was talking about and the keys,' said Chloe.

They exchanged looks. Erin could tell that Chloe didn't like the idea any more than she did.

Just then there was another rumble of thunder and a large raindrop fell from the sky. 'We'd better go home,' Chloe commented. 'It's not going to be safe to fly if there's a storm.'

'OK, I'll see you tomorrow at the stables!' Erin said. There was a louder crash of thunder and with a last wave they both dashed away.

Nine

The storm raged with thunderclaps so loud that they seemed to shake the clouds. It was very scary flying through the rain as lightning forked down to the ground. By the time Erin got home her heart was thudding in her chest and she was soaked through. Landing in her room, she quickly whispered, 'Stardust be gone.'

A heavy sinking sensation ran over her from her head to her toes. She blinked. Her sodden dress had turned back into her pyjamas, which were thankfully dry.

She dried her hair with a towel and got into bed. Outside, there was a loud crash of thunder and a flash of lightning again, but, exhausted from all the things that had happened that night, Erin immediately fell fast asleep.

'It's horrible out there!' Jo said, looking out of the window the next morning as Erin got herself some toast and jam for breakfast. The storm had passed, but the skies were still heavy with grey clouds and a continuous light drizzle was falling. 'Do you still want to go to the stables? I don't imagine you'll be allowed to ride today if it carries on like this.'

'I'll still go,' Erin said, looking out uneasily at the grey clouds. 'I can help clean tack and muck out and stuff, and I'm meeting Chloe there.'

Jo smiled. 'So how are you two getting on? She seems really nice.'

'She is,' Erin said, settling back in her chair, pleased it was just her and Jo in the kitchen. 'We're best friends now. We —'

Jake burst in. 'Where are my tennis shorts, Mum?'

'By the ironing board. Oh, Jake, don't!' Jo said as Jake picked up the orange juice and was about to drink it straight from the carton. 'Get a glass!' She turned back to Erin. 'Sorry, sweetheart. You were saying?'

'Just that Chloe's really nice.'

Jo smiled. 'I like Nicky, her mum, too.'

'Can Chloe and I have a sleepover one night this week?' Erin asked.

Before Jo could reply, the back door opened and Sam came in. He was wearing his running things and his hair was wet from the drizzle. 'Morning, squirt,' he said, grinning at Erin. 'Hey, Mum, any chance of bacon and eggs for breakfast?'

'Bacon and eggs?' Ben said, coming in from the little room off the kitchen where he had been watching a sporting channel in his dressing gown. 'I'll have some too.'

'And me. Where are my trainers, Mum?' Jake said, looking around.

'Boys, I'm trying to talk to Erin!' Jo said. She shook her head in despair as she looked at Erin. 'Of course you can have a sleepover. Just let me know what night and I'll talk it over with Nicky. Now, do you want bacon and eggs too?'

'No, thanks.' Erin put her plate in the dishwasher and escaped from the noisy kitchen. She did love her stepbrothers, but they were very loud when they were all in one room. She wondered what Chloe would make of them if she did stay over. *Maybe I'll ask if I can stay at hers!* she thought.

It was a cold, wet day at the stables and even Chloe seemed subdued. They didn't get many chances to be on their own, but Erin was sure Chloe was thinking about the night before. She couldn't stop thinking about it herself. How could Marianne hurt Tor like she did?

Power, thought Erin with a shiver. *Just because of power.* She shivered. They had to stop her. If only she wasn't the one who had to do the spell.

The air felt heavy with rain when the girls met on the beach that evening.

'Xanthe rang,' Chloe said. 'I sent her a mail this morning. She said dark spirits are very dangerous and we have to be *really* careful. We mustn't go near Marianne again.'

'But what about helping Tor and finding the hagstone with the hair?' Erin protested.

'Xanthe says it's too dangerous for us to go to Marianne's house. She's coming to stay at my house tomorrow and said she will decide what to do then – she says we're not to do anything about him until she's here.'

Erin felt a mixture of relief and frustration. It would be brilliant to have a grown-up to help them and not to feel they had to do it all on their own, but she wanted to free Tor as soon as possible. She didn't want to wait even a night.

'I was thinking we could ask if you could stay over at my house tomorrow,' Chloe went on. 'Then you'll be able to talk to Xanthe more, not just see her in the evening.'

'Brilliant,' Erin said eagerly. She looked around. 'So what are we going to do tonight?'

'Well . . .' Chloe hesitated. 'When we went into the feed room, the very first time we went to Marianne's house, I'm sure I saw some keys on a big red ring hanging on a hook opposite the door. They looked like the keys she had last night. Maybe we should go and see if they are the keys to the hut in the woods.'

'But Xanthe said we're not to go near Marianne's house,' Erin pointed out.

'It's not like we're going to the house, is it?' Chloe said persuasively. 'I'm sure it'll be safe. We can camouflage ourselves and just look through the window. We might not be able to go looking for the hagstone until Xanthe's here, but at least if we find the right keys that's a start.'

Erin nodded. She agreed completely.

They flew straight to Lookout Point. There was a light on in one of the downstairs rooms of the house.

'Look!' Erin said in a low voice.

'Maybe Marianne's in there. Let's check,' said Chloe. 'If she is, we know we're safe to look in the feed room.'

Erin nodded and, keeping themselves camouflaged, they flew cautiously towards the house. The window with the light on was open slightly and the curtains had not been drawn.

Marianne was inside, sitting at a large polished table, a piece of paper in her hand. She looked deep in thought and seemed to be speaking out loud to herself. Erin strained her ears to listen through the open window.

'He is too stubborn . . . too proud . . .' Marianne was muttering, looking down at the piece of paper. She read for a moment and then ran a hand through her hair. '*But one coming willingly lets the dark's power grow.*' She nodded slowly. 'Of course. It needn't be him. Just one with royal blood. Now, why didn't I think of that before?' Getting to her feet, she hurried out of the room.

'What was all that about?' Chloe whispered, mystified.

'I don't know,' Erin answered uneasily.

They both jumped as they heard the front door open and Marianne stalked out. She was wearing her cloak. Underneath it Erin could see the glint of her

pale-blue dress. Marianne took off into the skies and headed swiftly towards World's End.

An idea flashed into Erin's mind. 'Quick! Let's have a look around the house before she comes back!'

Chloe hesitated. 'But we don't know how long she'll be.'

'We'll just have a quick look,' urged Erin.

'But it will be like breaking in.' Chloe bit her lip.

'I know,' Erin said. 'But we have to help Tor, don't we? And that means going inside to find the hagstone.' She saw Chloe's troubled face. 'We're not going to be taking anything else and we have to find the stone. This could be the perfect chance, Chloe, but look, it's OK if you

don't want to come in – stay out here
and keep guard.'

'No, I'm coming in too,' Chloe said
immediately. 'I'm not letting you go in
on your own!'

The window was open just enough
for Erin to get her hand through to
unhook the catch and push it fully
open. 'Where shall we start?' Chloe said
as they squeezed inside.

'I don't know,' Erin whispered. Even
though she knew Marianne was out,
she felt the urge to stay as quiet as
possible. She had the uncomfortable
feeling that the house itself was
somehow watching them.

They looked around the room. There
were shelves and tables with things
piled on, strange things – old books, a

silver bowl, a glass bottle, a grey feather and some black cord.

'Look!' said Chloe, going to an old-fashioned bureau in one corner. On top of it were ten hagstones of different shapes and sizes. Erin hurried over with her. Maybe one of them would be the hagstone they needed!

But none of them had any hair wrapped round it.

Chloe gingerly opened the bureau. Inside there were lots of small drawers and shelves.

Erin's eyes fell on a box on the bottom shelf. It reminded her of her mum's box. It looked as if it was made from exactly the same type of dark wood. It was much smaller though. She took it out and opened the lid.

'Chloe!' she breathed. 'Look!'

There, nestling on a green baize lining, was a grey hagstone with a single hole. Through the centre of it three long strands of blonde hair were wound round and round.

'You've found it!' whispered Chloe.

Erin took it out, her fingers trembling slightly. 'It's just like Tor told me.'

'Let's take it and go,' Chloe said quickly

'We can't just leave the box empty,' Erin pointed out. 'If Marianne checks inside, she'll realize that someone has taken it and she'll know they would only have taken it if they were trying to destroy the rope.'

'But what can we do?' Chloe asked.

Erin studied the stone. It looked very

like the stone she had found on the
beach the first day she had seen the
cloud horses. She had that stone in her
pocket, but she didn't need it. She could
use any hagstone with a single hole in to
look at the cloud horses. She pulled it
out of her pocket. It really did look very
similar to the stone Marianne had used
– apart from one thing . . .

Erin quickly pulled three hairs from
her head and wound them round the
stone in her hand.

'Brilliant!' said Chloe. 'Your hair's exactly the same colour as Marianne's!'

'Now she might not realize it's gone,' Erin said. She slipped the stone into the box and tucked Marianne's stone into her pocket. They had got what they needed. 'Come on,' she said quickly. 'Let's get out of here right now!'

They flew out of the window and raced to Tor's building.

Erin touched the door. 'Tor! It's us! We've got the hagstone!' she whispered.

The sky stallion whinnied in delight. 'Where did you find it?'

'It was in the house,' Erin told him. 'Does this mean we can do the spell?'

'When we have a rope of bindweed,' Tor said. 'And the keys.'

'Well, we think the keys might be in

the feed room,' said Chloe. 'And there's loads of bindweed in my garden. I heard my dad going on about it.'

'Make a rope of it and bring it tomorrow night,' Tor instructed. 'If you can find the keys to let me out, I will tell Erin how to perform the unbinding spell.' He looked at her. 'It will be difficult, but I am sure you will be able to do it.'

'Tomorrow?' Erin said nervously.

'Yes,' Tor replied. 'You have done so well.' He snorted. 'Maybe tomorrow I will be able to return to the skies.'

'And then Marianne won't be able to hurt you any more,' Chloe said.

Tomorrow, the word echoed through Erin's head.

She only barely registered Tor

whinnying. 'You should leave now. The dark one has not been here tonight yet. She may come to see me at any time. Go!'

'OK. Bye, Tor!' Chloe exclaimed, flying upwards.

Erin didn't move.

'Come on, Erin!' Chloe said, flying back and pulling at her. 'Let's go!'

Thoughts racing, Erin followed her into the sky.

CHAPTER

Ten

When Erin got home, she placed
Marianne's hagstone on the window
ledge, but it made her feel odd seeing
the hair wound round it, so she covered
it up with a book.

She lay in bed, feeling far from
sleep. She was really pleased they had
got the hagstone, and relieved that
Xanthe was going to be there the next
night when she had to do the spell to
break the rope. But she couldn't stop

thinking about the magic she would have to do.

What if I get it all wrong? she thought worriedly. Tor had said the spell was going to be difficult. *What if I can't do it? I can't even make it rain or hail properly yet. How can I possibly do difficult weather-weaving magic?*

Sitting up, she took a hagstone from the box beside her bed. She turned it round in her hands a few times and then looked at the sky through the hole.

The horses looked darker at night, but she could still see them. They were all moving in different directions – heads tossing and half rearing as they wheeled around and occasionally lashed out at each other with hooves and teeth. They looked more restless and agitated than she had ever seen before.

A strange cloud shape near some trees caught Erin's eye. It was an almost circular cloud with a hole in the middle; she was suddenly reminded of the round stone at World's End. It looked just the same!

A foal was standing by it, staring at the hole. Something about this colt reminded Erin of Tor – the proud curve of his neck, the dark eyes rimmed by grey shadows, the prick of his intelligent ears. He was staring into the hole, almost as if he could see something.

Whatever he was seeing he didn't seem to like. He tossed his short mane

and swung round in a circle before
looking at the hole again. This time, he
half reared in agitation.

A mare came trotting over to him;
she was snow white and very beautiful.
Erin recognized her as the mare who
was usually bossing about the groups of
young horses and leading the other
mares and foals. Her dark eyes were
bright and her mane and tail were long
and silken. The colt nudged her
anxiously with his nose and then half
reared again.

Something was clearly troubling him.
Erin wondered what it was, but there
was no way of telling. Maybe he was
Tor's son, Mistral. He must be missing
his father. Determination flooded
through her.

I'll help Tor get back to you, she vowed, cradling the hagstone in her cupped hands. *However difficult it is, I'll do the unbinding spell. I will!*

By the next morning a fierce wind had built up. It was much too windy and wet to ride, but Erin and Chloe still hung around at the stables helping tidy the rug room and clean tack. Nicky and Jo had agreed to the sleepover and Nicky collected them at tea time.

As Nicky drove them back from the stables, Erin watched the rain pouring down. Water was spilling on to the roads from the surrounding fields. If the rain didn't stop soon, then there would be massive floods. The radio was on and

she could hear the weatherman on it
talking about the dreadful weather they
were having, issuing a flood warning
and telling people to take care.

They had just gone back to the
house when Xanthe arrived. Her long
blonde hair was tied back with a scarf
and she had a wide smile on her face.
She hurried through the wind and rain

to the doorway and kissed Nicky. Then she turned to the girls. 'Hi, Chloe!' She swept her goddaughter into a hug and then smiled at Erin. 'And you must be Erin.'

Erin nodded shyly. It was strange actually meeting Xanthe properly after hearing about her so much.

Xanthe leant down to kiss her cheek in greeting. 'We'll talk later,' she murmured in a voice only Erin could hear.

It seemed ages before she and Chloe got Xanthe on her own. First of all, Xanthe had a coffee and chat with Chloe's mum and dad, and produced a present for them – tickets to the theatre that evening and a night staying at a hotel.

'But we can't just go!' protested Nicky. 'What about Chloe – and Erin?'

'I can look after them,' said Xanthe. 'I know how stressed you've both been with the house move and, seeing as it's your wedding anniversary next week, I thought this would be the ideal early present.'

'It's wonderful, Xanthe! Thank you!' said Nicky in delight.

When Xanthe went upstairs to unpack her bag, Chloe and Erin finally got a chance to talk to her. As soon as they were in the spare room, Xanthe commented, 'Well, you two, it seems like a lot's been going on.'

'Loads,' Chloe said.

'Do you know what I'll have to do

for the unbinding spell?' Erin asked anxiously. 'Tor's told me that it'll be very difficult.'

Xanthe took her hands. 'I'm afraid I don't know any more than that myself. I wish I could do the spell for you, but only a weather weaver can work binding and unbinding magic of this sort. I will try to keep Marianne out of the way to give you time to perform the spell though, so at least you will not be in danger from her. Does she know that you are stardust spirits and that you have met Tor?'

'No,' Erin said.

'Good,' Xanthe replied, looking relieved. 'In which case she will not be suspecting that anyone is trying to free him.' Her eyes met Erin's. 'Try not to

worry,' she said softly. 'All you can do
is try your best and hopefully by the
morning the stallion will be free and
back in his cloud kingdom where he
belongs.'

When Chloe's parents left the house,
Xanthe helped the girls gather enough
bindweed from the garden to plait
into a long rope. The rain was starting
to slow down. By the time it was
dark and they turned into stardust
spirits it had finally stopped, but more
heavy clouds were already gathering
on the horizon and there was a
dangerous feel about the air. It
seemed charged with electricity.
Erin could feel it tingling across her
skin.

'There's Lookout Point,' Chloe
said to Xanthe as they approached
the house. 'Erin's gran used to live
there.'

'She would have been a weather
weaver too,' Xanthe said. 'Weather
weavers pass their abilities down
through the generations. You will have
come from a family of weather weavers,
Erin. Your mother would have been a
weather weaver as well.'

'My mum?' But deep down Erin realized she wasn't that surprised. Ever since she had found out about weather weavers, a part of her had wondered if her mum had been one too – if that was why she had kept a box of them and why she had kept the bit of paper in the box that talked about a dark one coming.

Xanthe nodded. 'The gift of weather weaving passes down the generations through the female members of the family. When all this is over, you must learn how to use your powers properly. They are very, very special. However, now let's concentrate on the night ahead.'

'The lights are on in the house,' Chloe said warningly.

'I wonder if Marianne is inside,'
Xanthe replied.

'Yes, look!' Chloe said as Marianne
appeared at one of the windows,
drawing the curtains.

'Excellent,' Xanthe said. 'I will go and
keep her talking. I will tell her there is
concern about the weather along the
coast and ask if she knows anything
about it. You must be as quick as you
can.' She smiled at them. 'Good luck!
And remember the important thing
with magic of any kind is to believe
you can do it. Believe it and it will
happen!'

She flew off. The girls raced to the
feed room and pulled open the door as
quietly as they could. The ring of keys
was still hanging opposite the door.

Chloe grabbed them and they flew straight to the woods.

There was an eager whinny from inside as if the sky stallion could sense them coming.

'Tor!' Erin gasped, reaching the door of the building. 'We're here and we've got everything!'

Chloe opened the door.

Tor stepped forward, his neck arched, his proud head held high. Erin reached out instinctively and then her hand dropped; he was not a tame horse to be petted. She stared at him in awe. He was wild, majestic, a king of horses.

'I'm ready to do the spell and break the rope.' Erin looked at the black rope round Tor's neck and reached to pull it off.

Tor jerked back. 'No!'

But he was too late; Erin's fingers had already closed round it. It burnt her like flames and with a sharp cry she yanked her hands back.

'What's the matter?' Chloe asked in alarm.

Erin stared down. Her fingers were red where she had touched it and she could already see three blisters forming. 'Look!'

Tor immediately breathed on her hand. Erin felt the sensation of snowflakes settling on her skin, soothing the burning, healing the blisters. 'I am sorry, Erin. But the rope cannot be removed until it is broken by the spell. I should have warned you sooner.'

Erin looked at the sores on his neck and bit her lip. 'How do I do the spell?'

'Unbinding magic is dangerous to perform,' Tor replied. 'You must use your powers as a weather weaver to enter a vision that will seem as real to you as real life. You must then do the unbinding in the vision. It will hurt and it will be hard.'

'Oh,' Erin said, swallowing.

Tor's dark eyes met hers. He raised his muzzle to her face, strength in his gaze. 'You are special, Erin. You will be able to do this.'

She felt his mane brush against her cheek, felt his breath on her hair, and courage flooded through her.

She lifted her chin. 'I won't let you down.'

Tor gave a low grateful whicker. 'Come,' he said softly. 'It is time.'

CHAPTER
Eleven

Tor plunged out of the hut. 'Clear the hagstones and make a circle with the bindweed as quickly as you can!'

Chloe and Erin did as he said, piling the hagstones up and laying the bindweed rope on the ground, tying the two ends together.

'What next?' asked Erin.

Tor stamped a hoof. 'First, you must pull a loose thread from the binding rope . . .'

'But that'll burn Erin, won't it?' interrupted Chloe.

'It will and I am sorry, Erin,' Tor said gently. 'But it is the only way.'

Erin thought of how much Tor must be hurting right now. 'I don't mind,' she said. 'What do I have to do when I have the thread?'

'Sit down with it in the bindweed circle and wind it through the hagstone. When it is all wound up, unwind the dark spirit's three hairs without breaking them. As the final hair comes free, you will enter a vision. In your vision, the bindweed circle will burst into flames. You must ignore it and begin to unwind the thread from the stone, all the time saying the spell: *unwind, untwist, free the bound one like this*. When you unwind the last of the thread, the vision will end. But remember —' Tor's voice took a note of urgency — 'if any words other than the spell pass your lips while you are in the vision, you will be trapped there. You must only speak the words of the spell.'

Erin could feel panic swelling inside her. How could she remember everything? 'Unwind, untwist, free the bound one like this,' she repeated.

Tor nodded. 'Be careful. It is very important that once you have started the spell you must not stop. If you break off, then the binding rope can never be broken. Do you understand?'

'Yes,' Erin answered, her lips dry.

Tor nudged her gently. 'Then use your magic, weather weaver.'

'Good luck,' Chloe said desperately. 'I know you can do it!'

Erin took a deep breath and took hold of a loose black thread in the rope round Tor's neck. It burnt her skin anew and she gasped.

Trying to ignore the pain, she pulled and the thread slid out of the rope. Erin ran into the circle with it and sat down.

Magic seemed to tingle through her from the stars and, as it did so, the pain from her fingers seemed to lessen slightly. Erin began to wind the thread through the hagstone, holding one end and taking the other through the hole and round and round. The thread cut into her fingers, but it wasn't burning in the same way. She gritted her teeth and thought about the pain Tor must be in with the rope round his neck all the time

Don't stop, she thought. *Keep going!*

Winding the last of the thread on, she tied the ends loosely and then began to unwind the three hairs – first one and then the next and then finally she started on the third.

The tingling feeling of magic increased and the edges of the world around her seemed to grow dark and blurry.

From the corners of her eyes she saw the white flowers of the bindweed seem to rise up and blaze with a bright light. She pulled the last hair away from the stone, and then suddenly the whole circle of bindweed burst into flame.

Erin cried out in alarm. Fire surrounded her. *It's a vision*, the word drummed in her head. *It's not real.*

But it *felt* real. She could feel the heat. Sweat broke out over her body. The flames seemed to be creeping closer. The woods, Tor, Chloe, everything had gone. There was just her and the flames and the hagstone in her hand.

Finding the loose ends of the thread, she tried to untie her own loose knot. But it was hard to concentrate; her eyes kept flicking back to the flames. They were definitely closer! Her breath grew short in her chest; panic started to rise through her.

Use your magic, Erin! Tor's voice seemed to ring in her ears.

Erin looked up at the sky – a cool, dark sea above. The stars were shining brightly, pinpricks of light and hope. Her panic ebbed, the ends came free and she started to unwind the thread from the stone. 'Unbind, untwist, free the bound one like this,' she whispered.

She could do this. She was a weather weaver. Tor had told her she was special. She put her trust in the cloud stallion.

'Unbind, untwist, free the bound one like this.' She pulled at the thread again. She was almost there. It was starting to burn her fingers again though, hotter and hotter.

'Unbind, untwist . . .' Her voice rose as she forced herself to block out the pain and think only of Tor. 'Free the bound one like this!'

On the last word she pulled out the end of the thread. There was a flaring of white light; she had a feeling of falling and suddenly Erin was out of the vision, sitting again in the clearing in the woods, the hagstone with the thread beside it in her hands. She blinked. She could see Chloe, her eyes wide with concern. She could see Tor, all his attention focused on her.

She'd done it. She had returned from the vision!

But just then the circle of bindweed round her — the real-life circle of bindweed — burst into flames. She screamed and heard Chloe scream too.

'Throw the thread into the flames, Erin!' Tor's voice rang out. 'Then use your stardust magic to quench the fire!'

Erin did as he said. As the thread burnt, the fire flared up, reaching towards her. She didn't have time for doubts . . .

'Rain be with me!' she yelled.

A second later, rain was pouring down, dousing the fire. With a sizzle, the flames died. The raindrops soaked her, streaming over her hair and face, soothing her heat-scorched skin.

'Rain be gone!' she gasped through the water.

The raincloud vanished. Erin's heart hammered in her chest. She looked at the circle of smoking, charred grass with just a few remaining bindweed leaves. Her eyes met Chloe's. At the same moment, a triumphant whinny rang through the clearing and Erin swung round to see Tor rearing up in the air.

'The rope!' Erin gasped, staring at his neck. 'It's gone!'

'You broke the spell!' Tor exclaimed. 'I am free!'

Erin jumped to her feet.

The next minute Chloe was hugging her. 'And you're OK, Erin! Oh, I'm so glad you're safe. It was horrible when you went into that trance. You cried out and then just went really still. I didn't know what was happening and then the fire . . .'

Tor plunged towards them and, as he did so, he seemed to change. The solid lines of his body blurred and faded, and in front of their eyes he grew bigger, filling the air of the clearing. He was no longer a stallion of flesh and blood, but a stallion made of swirling mist, his muscles rippling like scudding clouds, his mane and tail glittering like snow crystals caught in sunlight.

'What's happening to you?' Erin cried.

'My true cloud form!'

Tor reached them, and returned to his usual size. But his outline stayed cloud-like. 'Now the binding rope has gone, I can choose which form I take – real horse or sky horse. Oh, weather weaver . . .' He bent his head and touched his muzzle to her forehead. 'I knew you were special. Thank you.'

'Thank you for showing me how to use my powers,' Erin breathed, feeling a tingling coldness where his skin touched hers. She reached out to stroke his neck. It was like an icy mist, there but not there, soothing the last of the pain from her fingers.

'I must return to my kingdom,' Tor said. 'I need you to open the gateway for me – the gateway between this world and the cloud world. It is at World's End.'

'Is it the rock that looks like a hagstone?' Erin asked.

'The rock that *is* a hagstone,' Tor said.

But just then a figure in a silver dress came flying through the trees. She was holding her head and looked pale.

'Xanthe!' Erin exclaimed. 'Are you OK?'

'I'll be fine, don't worry,' Xanthe said, flying down.

'This is Xanthe, my godmother,' Chloe said quickly to Tor. 'She's here to help us.'

Xanthe landed lightly. 'Greetings, sky stallion.'

'Stardust spirit,' Tor said, bowing his head slightly.

Xanthe looked around. 'Is Marianne here?'

'No. We thought she was with you.'
Chloe frowned.

'She was,' Xanthe said. 'But then she
left. I tried to stop her, but her magic
was too strong.'

'I've broken the binding rope . . .'
Erin began.'

'Oh, well done!' Xanthe said.

But Erin knew there was no time for congratulations. 'Now I'm going to open a gateway so Tor can go back to the clouds.' She had no idea how she would do it, but she trusted Tor completely. He would tell her what to do. She shook her wet hair back.

'Let's not hang around here waiting for Marianne,' Chloe said. 'Come on!'

They flew out of the woods with Tor galloping below them, his outline constantly shifting and changing. No hedge or wall stopped him; he soared over them all, his mane and tail streaming out behind him like silver banners of mist.

Above them, the stars shone down out of a velvet-black sky. The moon was round and full.

As they flew, Xanthe explained what had happened at the house. 'At first I talked to Marianne, as I said I would, but she got impatient, said she had somewhere to be. She told me to leave and when I wouldn't she tried to use a stardust binding spell on me. I was ready and we fought. I managed to bind *her*, but she broke free when I wasn't expecting it and knocked me into the wall with a blast of wind. I banged my head and almost passed out. I can only imagine she must have been in a hurry to get to wherever she wanted to be, because, rather than trying to injure me further or take my stardust, she set off.'

'I wonder where she is,' said Erin, glancing around, half expecting to see

Marianne swooping towards them, but the sky was empty and silent. Very silent, Erin realized with a shiver. Almost as though the world was holding its breath.

They reached the cliff top. Tor swept down the path to the beach. Erin, Chloe and Xanthe flew down after him. The three rocks on the spit of land were silhouetted against the black sky, the round hagstone with moonlight gleaming through it and the two tall stones pointing upwards like fingers.

World's End, thought Erin, realizing what a good name it was for it — the place that was the end of one world and the beginning of another. Had the people who had named it known that?

'What do we have to do to open the gateway? What –'

She broke off with a gasp as a hooded figure stepped out of the shadows around the giant hagstone on to the shingle beach. It was Marianne!

Twelve

'You!' Marianne looked just as surprised to see them as they were to see her, Erin realized with a shock. The dark spirit's eyes swept over Tor's neck as he and the stardust spirits landed on the shingle in front of her. 'The binding rope!' she exclaimed in disbelief. 'It's gone!'

'Yes!' Tor's voice rang out. 'It has been destroyed.'

Marianne's gaze swung to Erin. 'You

did it! I didn't even know you had discovered your powers.'

Erin tensed, expecting Marianne to get angry, but to her surprise the dark spirit just stared coldly at her, then turned to look at Xanthe. 'Well, well. You came to create a distraction while the spell was performed. I see it all now.'

Xanthe met her gaze. 'It is true. The stallion has been freed and he will return to the skies now. You have no business here any longer, dark spirit.'

'We're going to open the gateway and let him through, and you're not going to stop us!' Chloe exclaimed.

Xanthe pulled Chloe protectively towards her.

Marianne shrugged. 'I agree I'm not

going to stop you from opening the gateway, child. In fact . . .' A smile curved the corners of her lips. 'I'm going to open it *for* you.'

'What?' Erin and Chloe both burst out.

Marianne turned to the hagstone and moved her left hand in a circle, muttering a word. The air in the hole immediately began to shimmer with a silver light. Tor moved towards it instinctively – then hesitated.

Marianne looked at him. 'The gateway is open, sky stallion. You may return if you wish. I do not need you any more. I have other plans!' She laughed triumphantly. 'And your presence here can only help me in those!'

She turned to the stone and for a

moment seemed to be addressing
something through it rather than them.
'Can you see him?' she called. 'Can you
see him here?'

'Father!' a voice echoed back.

There was a flash of bright white
light and suddenly a colt came jumping
through the hagstone, a colt made of
clouds. His outline was slightly blurred,

his body changing very slightly every second in size and shape. It was the same long-legged foal Erin had seen the night before.

'Mistral!' Tor whinnied in alarm.

Marianne stepped forward swiftly, pulling out a hagstone with a chip of rock caught in the centre of its hole. She reached out and touched it to the grey colt's head, muttering a string of dark words.

To Erin's horror, the colt gave a startled whinny that was cut off as he seemed to be sucked into the hole in the rock, the cloud that made him swirling in until it was gone.

'No!' Tor reared up. At the same moment, Xanthe lifted her hand to shoot magic at the dark spirit, but it was too late. Marianne had disappeared, the stone in her hands.

'Reveal!' Xanthe shouted desperately. But nothing happened.

A cold laugh echoed from the cliff top above them. They swung round and looked to see Marianne standing there, the wind tossing back her long hair. She pointed at Xanthe. 'Bind her!' she snapped. Xanthe suddenly seemed to freeze in mid-air.

Marianne looked directly at Erin. 'You thought you had won by breaking the binding spell, but I do not need Tor any longer. He was too stubborn, too difficult. Any sky horse of royal blood can be used to control the weather from Earth and so I found another. In fact, by bringing the stallion here you

helped me. As soon as the foal saw his
father, he came through the gateway
willingly.' She held up the stone. 'Now I
will use *him* to control the skies. Just as
it is written in the stars!' With a
gloating expression on her face, she
quoted four lines:

> '*When the dark one returns, the door*
>   *shall be reopened*
> *And danger will threaten all living*
>   *below.*
> *If the binding is broken, they can be*
>   *protected,*
> *But one coming willingly lets the dark's*
>   *power grow.*'

Marianne drew herself up to her full
height. 'You may have broken the

binding, but my power has indeed grown.' And, with that, she vanished.

In the same instant, Xanthe broke free.

'Quick! Let's go after her!' Chloe cried, flying into the air.

'No, Chloe!' exclaimed Xanthe. 'Marianne is too powerful. We cannot stop her by chasing her now.'

Chloe stopped reluctantly.

'We need to wait and plan,' said Xanthe. 'We need to gather our strength.'

Tor pawed the ground. 'You are right,' he said, but he did not sound as if he liked it. Looking at the anger on his face, Erin was sure he wanted to go flying after Marianne straight away.

Chloe flew down again. 'What did all those words she said mean?'

'It sounded like a prophecy,' Xanthe said grimly.

'I've heard those words before,' said Erin, her heart thudding. 'They're on a piece of paper that used to belong to my mum.'

'It must be a weather-weaving prophecy,' said Xanthe. 'Marianne must have realized that if a sky horse came through the gateway willingly then she would become more powerful. It sounds as if she has been using her magic to cast visions of Tor being mistreated into the cloud world, knowing that his son would feel compelled to come through to try to help him.'

'And then we helped her by coming here tonight,' said Erin slowly.

'And now my son is her prisoner, caught within a trapping stone, unable to break free,' Tor said heavily.

Chloe looked at him. 'What will you do now? Will you go back to the cloud world?'

'Yes,' said Erin. 'We can find Mistral and you can tell us what to do, how to free him.'

'Your herd needs you, sky stallion,' said Xanthe, looking up at the stormy sky.

'I cannot go,' Tor said in frustration. 'To free Mistral after he has been trapped in the stone, I will need to speak his sky name. A sky horse's secret name must not be spoken by any apart from those from the cloud world, or the sky horse will become earthbound forever.'

'But what about the storms?' protested Erin. 'If you stay here, then what's going to happen?'

'All hope is not lost. If you will help me by learning to use your weather-weaving powers, we will be able to control the weather and calm the skies from here,' said Tor. 'But I will need you to work your magic.'

'I'll do anything!' said Erin fervently. '*Anything!*' She looked at the giant hagstone – the gateway to another world. She could almost see the faint outline of the colt, ears pricked, as he had burst through it and landed on the shingle.

Tor touched her shoulder with his

muzzle. 'Thank you. Maybe together we can defeat the dark one.'

They flew back to Chloe's house. Tor said he would stay in the woods. Now Marianne had the foal she would not try to capture him again.

Back at Chloe's house, Xanthe made them some hot chocolate. As Erin

sipped the froth off the top of her mug
and nibbled at a biscuit, she sighed. She
felt shaken. Tor should have returned to
his cloud kingdom. She'd done the
magic and the binding rope was broken,
but now that Marianne had Mistral he
still couldn't go back.

Xanthe squeezed Erin's shoulder as if
she could read her thoughts. 'You
should be really proud of what you did
tonight, Erin. Working the spell to
break the binding rope must have been
incredibly hard, and to do it when you
have only just become a weather
weaver . . . well, that's amazing.'

'It didn't help though, did it?' Erin
said unhappily.

'Erin!' Xanthe moved round so she
could look into her eyes. 'Of course it

helped! Tor is free. He can be either his earth form or his cloud form and now that he is no longer controlled by Marianne he will be able to work with you to manage the weather in the skies, stopping the storms and then freeing Mistral. If he had still been bound by Marianne, then he would not have been able to do that. He said he will tell you what to do tomorrow.'

'I can't believe you're going to get to work with Tor to control the weather,' Chloe said. 'That's so cool!' She shook her head wonderingly. 'It really has been an amazing few days, hasn't it?'

It had. Erin realized that just a week ago she hadn't heard of stardust, hadn't known about weather weavers, had had no idea there were horses in the skies and absolutely no idea she could do magic. So much had happened – good bits, bad bits, and two of the best bits, she realized, had been making friends with Chloe and the strong bond she now felt with Tor, a weather-weaving bond that linked her and the stallion across the wide, dark night.

'You really were brilliant this evening, Erin,' Chloe said. 'Xanthe's right. It would have been great if we could have got Tor back to the clouds, but the most important thing is that he's free and Marianne can't hurt him any more with that horrible rope.'

Erin nodded slowly. 'And we *will* set Mistral free too. We're not going to let Marianne beat us.'

'No way!' declared Chloe.

Their eyes met and Erin felt a warmth spread through her that had nothing to do with the chocolate she was drinking. 'Definitely no way,' she said, lifting her chin with a smile.

It all started with a Scarecrow

Puffin is well over sixty years old.
Sounds ancient, doesn't it? But Puffin has never been
so lively. We're always on the lookout for the next big
idea, which is how it began all those years ago.

Penguin Books was a big idea from the mind of
a man called Allen Lane, who in 1935 invented
the quality paperback and changed the world.
**And from great Penguins, great Puffins grew,
changing the face of children's books forever.**

The first four Puffin Picture Books were hatched in 1940 and the
first Puffin story book featured a man with broomstick arms called
Worzel Gummidge. In 1967 Kaye Webb, Puffin Editor, started the
Puffin Club, promising to **'make children into readers'**.
She kept that promise and over 200,000 children became
devoted Puffineers through their quarterly installments of
Puffin Post, which is now back for a new generation.

Many years from now, we hope you'll look back and
remember Puffin with a smile. **No matter what your age
or what you're into, there's a Puffin for everyone.**
The possibilities are endless, but one thing is for sure:
whether it's a picture book or a paperback, a sticker book
or a hardback, **if it's got that little Puffin
on it – it's bound to be good.**